Eenie Meenie Mynie Murder
by C. D. Moulton

Murders of several persons with no known connections. What was the motive? Pick up´the phone book and make a stab at the page, then kill the name under your finger? Eenie, meenie mynie murder?

Contents

About the author

CD Moulton has traveled extensively over much of the world both in the music business, where he was a rock guitarist, songwriter and arranger and in an import/export business. He has been everything from a bar owner to auto salvage (junkyard) manager, longshoreman to high steel worker, orchid grower to landscaper, tropical fish farmer to commercial fisherman. He started writing books in 1983 and has published more than 350 books as of January 1, 2023. His most popular books to date are about research with orchids, though much of his science fiction and fantasy work has proven popular. He wrote the CD Grimes, PI series, and the Det. Nick Storie series, Clint Faraday series, and many other works.

He now resides in Gualaca, Chiriqui, Panamá, where he writes books, plays music with friends, does research with orchids and medicinal plants. He has lately become involved in fighting for the rights of the indigenous people, who are among his closest friends, and in fighting the extreme corruption in the courts and police in Panamá.

He offers the free e-book, *Fading Paradise*, that explains what he has been through because of the corruption.

CD is the discoverer of the Chadam Protocol for curing cancer.

Facebook page Ambrosia peruviana for cancer.

<u>*A Puzzle*</u>

Det. Lt. Sam Rankin, Violent Crimes, plopped down into the semi-comfortable chair at his desk, slid open the drawer to take out the growing file. He groaned out of the chair and went to the urn to pour himself a cup of luke-warm almost-drinkable coffee, went back to the chair, sat, took a sip, and made a sour face.

He was tired. More than just tired. He was bordering on exhaustion.

Three murders in three days. This made five in three weeks.

Was it a single killer, some kind of plan among two or more, or an organization ... what?

There didn't seem to be a connection among the victims. The only clue they had that they were connected was a white gardenia flower left on each body.

What was the significance? Did they have to find who had a gardenia plant at his house? That was stupid. There was a hedge of those wood-flower gardenias in the park and every fourth or fifth house had them.

He picked up the individual reports;

Lacey Deana McLarin, W F (g?) 24 114 ntrl blnd/bl 5'10"sngl apt fitness instructor slfempl

She was the first. Found in the parking lot behind LDM Gym. Garrote. She owned and ran the place. No complaints, no record, except parking tickets. Two in three years. Not member of groups, except virtual groups on Facebook and Twitter. Had a blog. Bank account 1st Fed in company name and personal account other in different bank. Citi. Reg. Rep. There was a question of whether she was gay. Agnostic.

Sam was methodical. He had checked it before, but went to the blog again. It was mostly blah. Advice on fitness programs and advertising her business. A few short notes about health and medicine. One semi-argumentative exchange because she said a post about the horrors of GMO was too extreme, and that more testing was necessary before she made up her mind. The poster said she was stupid. The evidence was an avalanche and clear.

The only one that was confrontatious at all. Gardner Flores.

He wrote that down, thought a minute, then went to Facebook. There were several Gardner Flores members. All but one had nothing on his profile. That one was, apparently, in the UK.

Franklin George Dennis, B-L 62 178 br/gry

5'11" wdwd hm AC tech

No record. Found in backyard of home. Stabbed/3. Bank account, personal HSBC. SD w/stocks in Monsanto, Bayer, Wal*Mart. Reg. Rep. Used comp for e-mails and some download movies (XX).

He was widowed and downloaded a couple of porn movies. He was a black-Latino, and a republican?

Well there were some. Islam.

Daniel Vernon Whiteside. W M (g) 31 150 blnd/br 5'8" sngl. hm/rnt stkbrkr

He was gay. McLarin might have been. Check on Dennis. Could be the connection.

Found in car (2014 BMW) by Riverside Park. Shot in the head. (Slug and case recvrd. Colt .45) Had a company and a large personal bank account. Lots of stocks. Conservative politics. Protestant. On internet in groups and shared blogs. Went to a couple of gay X video sites, but not often.

Check on those movies. They were on the memory stick from Dennis's computer.

Definitely and absolutely not gay. Disgustingly not gay.

Sam liked some erotic things, but the crotch shots and explicit actions on those disgusted him.

Well, if it didn't have anything to do with his case, it was none of his business.

He now didn't have a motive suggestion.

Republicans? Whiteside was conservative, but probably not republican. He didn't have anything at all. They were from different parts of the city and shared nothing else that Sam could see.

He refilled his coffee mug and sat.

Lilian (NMI) Rose, neé Lillian Kate Mills. W(dk) F 37 122 rd (ntrl brn)/hzl 5'7" apt (prst).

Had a big bank account and a drawer full of stocks, plus a lot of expensive jewelry. Her record was long, but all petty. A prostitute. She was found in her apartment. Blunt instrument. Spent a lot of time on the internet, chatting. Kicked out of a couple groups for being a troll.

The latest, Wo Lu Lastinger. Oriental, from Taiwan. F 49 155 bl/br 5'5" hm own supermarket. Big bank accounts, several in company names, three personal, a large stock portfolio, wdw. Found behind restaurant Lu Wan. Blunt instrument. Apolitical. Non-religious. Time on the internet was limited to consulting with relatives in New York, Los Angeles, San Francisco and Orlando. All business.

Connections in that?

Upper middle class to wealthy. All had bank

accounts, all had stocks.

Sam was used to the trite "Puzzle with a couple of pieces missing" saying. This was a puzzle with all *but* a couple of pieces missing. He had that they were well-to-do to rich and they owned stocks.

What could there be in that? Anything he could expand, to get a direction of some sort?

He read over the lists of stocks. What he supposed was normal. He didn't know much about that. It was over his income bracket. He did note that all of them had control stock in three companies, but most weren't on but one or two portfolios.

Monsanto, which he supposed most stock-oriented investors had, because of the news lately. Bayer, which was also a good investment, because it was huge in drugs. Lily, ditto. Those were the three all of them had.

So did thousands of other people in that state alone. It didn't seem a likely place to look.

Could it be personality? Was it someone who was easily offended and all of them ... they were all upper income people. And Republican or conservative. He would have to check on their personalities. These had made remarks that had pushed someone over the edge?

He had friends of all of them on lists. He could

possibly manage this from the phone. He got the list from McLaren and made a call:

"Mrs Williams, I have a couple of questions about Miss McLaren. They are about her personality. We are trying to find a common ground among several murders, and it could be from a personality trait."

"She was bisexual, and didn't hesitate to let you know, if that's what you mean."

"No. We know that. It's how she treated people who were not as ... well off ,,, as her."

"Well, it was pointless to try to borrow from her, and she would tell beggars to get a job, if that's what you mean."

"Yes. More or less. It's altogether possible she made that kind of remark to the wrong person."

"Oh, dear!"

"Thank you for your help." Sam rung off. The tone and word selection told him that one was the same. She would make cutting remarks. Maybe now she'd think first.

He checked the next one and called, but got no answer. He called another number.

"Your quarter! What?"

"Mr. Sutton, I am Sam Rankin, with the police. I'm investigating the murder of Mr. Dennis. We may have a direction, at last, but it's pretty thin.

"I have to know something about his relations

with other people, particularly how he treated those with less."

"Call me Bill. He was an ass to anyone who didn't think money was the most important thing in life. He was alright away from the subject, except he would rant about those goddamned liberals and their give everything away to the bleeding hearts and bums in society."

"People seem to be able to compartmentalize their minds. Thanks."

"That's it?"

"What?"

"Oh! I see! Somebody he ranted against wanted to shut him up – and did?"

"It's altogether too possible."

"Got anybody specific in mind?"

"It's down to a couple million suspects."

Bill laughed and they chatted a moment.

So! Maybe he did have a direction, with the caveat he mentioned to Bill.

He made a couple of notes, then called the next one.

"Miss Ames? I'm Sam Rankin, police. I'm calling to find a few facts about Mr. Whiteside. Personality traits. We may have found a direction for the investigation."

"Yes?"

"It's about how he treated those with less. Monetarily, that is."

"He treated everybody the same. The money made life easier. He came from nothing and made his on his own initiative, so he knew the obstacles and could relate."

"So he wouldn't make a remark to a beggar or anything on that order?"

"No. Within reason, he always tried to help people. He would offer to help in education or to find employment, but understood how difficult it could be when one has no base from which to operate. He was a very good person. He believed in the United States, first, and was concerned with world health. He backed research in cancer and epidemic diseases. He would say how sick the world was when his biggest returns on investments were from drug companies, but supposed it was necessary if any progress was to be made at all."

"Thank you – I think."

"You think?"

"It blows big hole in my theory."

"That it was some beggar who was trying to rob him?"

"No. He had more than a thousand dollars in his pocket and that Rolex was worth four thousand dollars. We know robbery wasn't behind it."

"I rather imagine not."

Sam sighed and rang off. There went his motive.

He tried the next one.

"Miss Lavonne? I'm Sam Rankin, with the police. We are investigating the death of Miss Rose, and would appreciate you cooperation. There is a chance her personality is involved in the motivation of her killer. I need to know..."

"She was a total bitch. Next question?"

"That about covers it. Thanks!"

"Anytime. You sound sexy. Maybe we could get together and discuss police matters?"

"Ah! She was a business competitor?"

"You could say."

"I just did."

"You're fun! Why'nt dja come up 'n sue me sometime?" They both laughed. She did seem to be a fun type.

Well, that's just business. He chatted a little more, then rang off.

Maybe Whiteside was for another reason.

He called the last one.

"Mr. Wang, I'm Sam Rankin, with the police, investigating the murder of Mrs. Lastinger. There is a possibility her murder was connected to a personality difference.

"I need to know how she reacted to people who had less, who might have begged or something."

"She was never around those people. She was a very private person."

He didn't know what else to ask, so thanked him and rung off.

Well, that one went nowhere!

Sam turned over in the bed and glanced at the clock on the wall. 5:42 AM.

He answered the phone. "Yes? Sam Rankin here."

"Sam? Jan. We've got another body for you. Riverview Drive, number three A. Apartment. Some kind of poison, but the flower's here."

Jan was Janet Jameson, his partner, most of the time. She just got off vacation yesterday, but she had kept up with the case.

"Hmm. That doesn't seem to fit with ... I'll be there in about fifteen or twenty."

"Roger."

He got up and threw on yesterday's clothes, then headed for his car.

The one clue he had was that they were all more than comfortable, financially. Riverview didn't fit with that. While it was a long way from a slum, it was lower income middle class.

The CSI van was in the drive. Sam talked to Will Burns, chief investigator. He said the poison was one of those fast organics. He would know which one after the lab reported. Jan said to hold up transporting until Sam looked over the scene.

"Anything to see?"

Will shook his head. "No."

Sam nodded and went inside and up. He was surprised at how nice the apartment was, and at a picture hanging over the sofa. He didn't know a lot about art, but he could see that one was way up there. He touched it to feel the texture of the oil paint.

"It's insured for two hundred grand," Janet said, coming into the room. "Hi. I'm back, which you might have figured."

"Two hundred grand, in this section? What? A nutcase recluse? This place is class."

"He was owner of this and the two buildings across the street. Norton Levy. He also owns a lot of stocks and bonds or whatever. There's a safe in the den, through that door, that was open. I'd say several million dollars in stocks. There're fourteen gold bars and nine silver. He has some diamonds and such. One big emerald – the insurance papers are there – worth one point eight mil. If I thought I could get away with it, I would be away with it!

"He has a computer in there that's set on the stock market. He spent a lot of time in there.

"The one who found him, Kyle Sands, says he

was a nutcase about that stock. He spent ten hours or more a day in that den. He was in constant contact with some very big biggies in some of the corporations he was involved with. He erased all that correspondence except the parts that went into the records.

"Sands is his personal secretary. He came to work at his usual time, five, and found him."

"Poison? How delivered?"

"Delivered, I guess. He had all meals prepared by the Chef Alonzo, which he owned.. Breakfast at four thirty, so he could be ready when Sands got here."

"Cripes! What does the deliveryman have to say?"

"Haven't had time yet. You can check around, then we'll go to the restaurant to interview our prime suspect."

"Yeah, but suspected of what?"

"Getting up at an ungodly hour to deliver food to a money nut."

"Well, we can get a sure conviction for that!" She gave him the finger.

They checked together, but there simply wasn't anything to find that hadn't already been photographed and listed. They headed for the restaurant.

"All I know, they gave me the tray from the kitchen and I took it to him," Tom Whitmore, the deliveryman said. "Same thing every morning except Sunday. Gail takes it Sundays. He doesn't get up until eight on Sundays because the stock market is closed or something."

"You got along with him well?" Jan asked.

"As well as anyone. He opened the door and had me put the tray on the rack and watched me like he thought I was going to steal the silverware or something. Usually didn't say shit. Only one I ever worked for who didn't even say 'Thanks' or something. Christmas, he gave me a whole twenty bucks bonus for bringing the shit six mornings a week for a year without even a vacation.

"Well, we all know you have to use the jaws of life to get a nickel out of his hand."

"Okay. So the tray was never out of your sight from when you left here until you left it on the rack in his apartment?" Sam asked.

"No. I mean, I put it in the truck and came in for the other early deliveries. Two trips, but that was like three minutes each time, then he was the first delivery."

"There was a thermal box ... unless the poison was put in here in the restaurant, it could only be during two three minute periods. Is the truck in sight of where you got the food to put in it at all times?"

"Huh?"

"Yeah. Didn't make sense to me either."

"I know what you mean." He grinned. "It's out the door and to the left. You can see it as soon as you get out the door, but not from inside."

"So the next question is obvious. Was there anyone out there that you saw?" Jan asked.

He looked thoughtful. "No, but there could be someone in the cars. I never pay any attention to them. They're just the ones who work here that early. The place doesn't open for breakfast until a quarter to six."

They went inside to the kitchen, checked what they could there, talked to several of the cooks and the head chef – who didn't come in for breakfast, so they called him – then left. The employees had never met Levy

"Somebody who knew the routine and waited in a car to put something in the box," Jan said. Sam nodded.

"You look lost in another universe," Jan accused, grinning. "What?"

"Jan, what if the others were killed just to hide that Levy was the target all along?"

Jan raised an eyebrow.

"The others were comfortable. One was rich. She owned a restaurant here and a couple in California, or her family did. That could be the connection. Levy is worth, according to these papers Will gave me, more than forty million dollars. He was so tight ... no one ever got a penny from him. We have to see who inherits, and how much. Just from what we've seen so far, I would bet even money he held his wealth over everybody's head. He was a bit of a control freak and was as greedy as anybody I've ever come across.

"That emerald you like so much made me wonder why he had it. It's something that ... tells me a woman is involved, somehow. He sure as hell didn't buy that thing for himself, and it's too slow an investment for his type.

"We have to spend whatever time it takes going over everything about him. There wasn't a picture or letter or any mention of family there. That's sort of strange, don't you think?"

"I talked about that with Sands. He didn't have any family Sands knew about. He once dated a woman, but decided it was too risky and expensive to get married.

"I wonder if that emerald was the thing that made him think marriage was too expensive?"

Sam nodded and sighed. "We might as well get on with it. Sands contacted the law firm about the will or whatever, but he can't find which one has anything like that. All his law firms are about the business."

"The safe?"

"There are a lot of folders we haven't gone through yet. There were a couple of memory sticks in a locked box in the safe. That makes me wonder. Why have a steel lock box inside a safe that big?"

"How did you open the box? He had a key somewhere?"

"That's the funny thing. It was a cheap little lockable file box. Thirty seconds with a bent paper clip and it just happened to fall open in my hands."

"One day you'll get caught. Are they in evidence?"

"Yeah. I'll get them."

She went back to the evidence room. Sam poured a mug of coffee and took a sip. He made a face. *They could have used this coffee to kill him!*

Jan came back with the memory sticks. He put one in the USB port and brought up the index. It was all about decisions with the companies he owned big blocks of stock in. He didn't mind giving orders. He had enough others to back up what he wanted, and he did have a reputation for turning a profit from what seemed like a hopeless deal.

There was a section labeled "Lab Reports." He opened it to read a few things. Jan gave him a raised eyebrow when he whistled. "What?"

"... this was shown to have some negative effects after repeated exposure to the product. It has indications of a serious carcinogenous nature, and can also cause sterility. We can't know if this is a temporary effect until further tests are completed.."

"And?"

"He then sent a message that the tests made by Dr. Carter and Dr. Bennington had been contaminated and were declared non-useful. The product was to be put on the market immediately. He also said to restate the tests without the contaminant. This was to be done by deleting the two paragraphs that stated those effects were noted."

"But ... wouldn't the one who made the report challenge it?"

Sam grunted and read further. He whistled again. "Jan! Two weeks later he wrote that the unfortunate accident where Dr. Carter and Dr. Bennington were killed when a truck ran them off the road by the dam wouldn't interfere with the project because it had been shown their tests were contaminated – and referred to the report where he stated the tests had been contaminated and offered no corroboration!"

"I don't see ... Jesus Christ! Was that accident a bit too convenient?!"

"No. It was a hell of a long way past convenient! I want to go back over a couple of those ... no. I want to find what he referred to a couple times.

"Jan, I think he killed those two doctors, or had them killed. I really do! If it was someone from the families of one of those doctors, I won't find evidence against them for him. I will for the others. That would make them no better than him.

"Every time I think we've found the lowest a person can go, we find someone worse."

"There's one thing we have to do, and right now! We have to get that product off the market!"

"But it's just referred to as 'the product' here. We don't know which one it is."

"We have to see what product that company put on the market then. We also have to see what other products they or anyone else involved with him have the same kind of thing behind them.

"Sam, I'm calling in a federal crew to go over these memory sticks."

Sam thought. "Make copies. Don't let anyone know you did. Those companies can stop any investigation, and by the method Levy used to stop challenge to this one. It's no longer a joke that Washington is owned, lock, stock and barrel, by big corporations."

Jan shivered and nodded. "This is about to get hairy, isn't it?"

Sam took a deep breath. "Yeah."

"What if this isn't the real reason? What if there's something else that will smack us in the puss?"

"If there's another body, we don't have ... what we thought. It won't change what we've found here. It may give us a motive to work from. I did spot something I think may be important."

"What?"

"Every one of the victims had control stock in three big corporations. The very same corporations that are in the news, at least, on the net."

"Then I still don't get it. What are the murders about? Somebody trying to get their stocks? We would know who pretty fast, if that's the case."

"I don't ... maybe a reply to ... I think, just maybe, I'm starting to get an idea.

"Jan, we have to find the significance of gardenias! The answer *has* to be there, some-how."

Jan looked thoughtful, then nodded.

<u>*Why Gardenias?*</u>

"I've looked up gardenias on the internet until I'm bleary-eyed," Jan complained. "I can tell you where they come from, that coffee is a close relative, there are two hundred forty species. How to grow them, that they like acid soil, that some varieties like full sun, but most like partial shade, that they like a lot of water, but also want to be well-drained, that many varieties are trees. I can tell you the variety here is *Gardenia lucida* or *gumminifera* ... but I can't tell you why they are significant to this case."

"I've been looking up clubs or organizations that have any connection, outside of garden clubs and such. Nothing that tells me anything.

"There's significance in some ... they are often used in ... I've seen something close around here.... Jan, isn't there a little private cemetery out on Eastfork Road that's called Gardenia Something?"

"No. I think you mean Memories of Peace. It's a private cemetery for the ultra-rich from the River Heights area. It has a big gardenia logo ... and these are all upper end and wealthy. It's a symbol, a message to the rich. Somebody is knocking off rich people?"

"Only rich people who hold control stock in three companies. I do think it's a message to those people. There are hundreds, if not thousands, of people who have stocks in those companies."

"There may be hundreds, but not thousands, with control stock."

"It would have to be connected to something about those companies. There was a lot of publicity on the net about them recently. Monsanto is banned in a bunch of countries because the countries' scientists have claimed their products cause all kinds of things, from autism to cancer. This country is trying to pass some kind of law or treaty or whatever that makes it illegal to put the products from Monsanto on the labels of foods. I haven't paid it much attention.

"Maybe somebody whose kids have autism ... that was the drug companies. Monsanto is the cancer, more. Maybe somebody whose wife or mother or something got cancer?"

"I think I'm going to spend a few more hours on the net, researching exactly what's going on with that. I'll take the drug companies, you take Monsanto."

Jan was looking at the screen as she spoke. She did a Google on Monsanto. She whistled.

"What?"

"Monsanto. You ain't gonna find it easy! There are twenty four million two hundred thousand references!"

She went through the first five pages. "It looks like Monsanto puts a lot of things on the net to fill the pages. They're still more than half negative. There's even an international organization called Millions Against Monsanto. Several groups.

"I'll leave them to you."

She Googled Bayer, which was one of the drug companies mentioned. She'd known about Bayer Aspirin all her life.

Bayer was in a lot of hot water over their vaccinations. If one percent of what was charged was true, she could join the opposition.

Two hours later, she looked up to see Sam pouring another cup of coffee. "Is what you're finding leading to anything?"

Sam grimaced. "If ten percent is true, and there's more than that we know is true, I'd sorta like to help our killer out a bit, particularly if any of that crap affected his family or whatever."

"Well, this kind of thing can get blown way

out of proportion, but what I'm seeing ... they could be charged with war crimes. Even the Nazis didn't go that far, and it's all, it would seem, about money."

"Yeah. That's what convinces me about some of it. The greed ... it was like Levy was the clone of all the others."

"Yes. I've got a chilling bit of inference about something that could be directly behind it.

"Did you know that eight holistic doctors have been murdered or died suspicious deaths, all of whom were exposing those drug company's practices?"

"Well, that's a possible coincidence."

"In Florida. In the past three weeks. Five others are missing."

"*What*?! What have we gotten into, here?"

"They get short notices in the newspapers or on TV, then it passes on to racist issues and flags and sex changes. Everyone charges that the big stockholders in the drug companies own the media, and things are shut up.

"Sam, where's there's that much smoke, there's a conflagration!"

"I'm beginning to believe it, but we have to go slow. It's a pretty organized campaign, so we can't go by numbers and statistics here."

"We can go by scientific reports and lab results

that are authenticated, and there are thousands of them! Literally!"

"I'm doing that right now. I go to some of the things mentioned on blogs. A lot of them have links with scientific research organizations. I can read the original papers. Those have peer reviews by the hundreds. It's gotten scary beyond ... Jan, we can't accept a lot of this, but mainly because it's become an emotional issue. It's exaggerated. I've found some links in the papers that refer to studies that were debunked. It's a mess.

"I was just going to a link ... here. About a paper that claimed Monsanto knew about the dangers of some of its products for years. Dr. Mamamoto, with CenSciRev. Let's see, there is a reference to a refutation by Dr. Vilaine and Dr. Gordons ... from ... But that's a Monsanto lab!

"Jan, the damned legislature took the word of Monsanto's own so-called scientists against a world-renowned facility? Why would they? This is ridiculous!"

"I've run across a lot of charges of corruption. It's just another one on a *very* long list. Sam, one of these sticks seems to be about stock-holders' meetings. It's video-recorded. Levy went to it every year. I'm going to run it. It might tell us something. Considering those doctors, what if he said or did something at the last meeting, two months ago, that would lead to Bayer being exposed for ... what they are?"

"Shit! We don't *need* this!"

"I'm going through with this. If you want out, I understand. I might be setting myself up to be the next accident victim."

"You know me better. I'm in. All the way!"

They went back to an evidence investigation chamber. Jan put the stick into a USB port and clicked on 6/15/15. It opened with the meeting discussing a subsidiary, a chemical company, being called to order. Finances were discussed for almost an hour, then a new product was discussed. They called in several of their scientists who were testing it. Three said it didn't have any negative effects in the short term they had discovered. One said the long term experiments showed some disturbing features. One said it was too broad-spectrum. It was an automatic overkill that would damage the ecology of an area by killing all the needed organisms.

They promised to investigate that, immediately. As soon as the man left the room, they discussed how to shut him up. They called in a man who was supposed to be supervising the labs. He said he had a personal opinion that Dr.

Kilgarten was faking evidence. Levy took the floor to ask a few questions.

Q: Do you have any written or video proof?

A: Not at the moment. I can arrange it by tomorrow, I think. I do have a lot of videos with him ... you know what I mean?

Q: Yes. Please arrange for that information to be delivered to my office as soon as you have it ... arranged. We can fire him and discredit him, then his reports will be ignored.

The meeting then turned to ways to stop the negative publicity they were getting lately. Another three countries had banned their products.

Then another subsidiary was discussed. Jan turned it off.

"Well, I think I'll testify that whoever offed him was at my house for the past four of five days and nights, and had not left at anytime for any reason," Jan said. "I can't remember ever being this disgusted.

"I want to check the computers and phone records of all the victims. I think we'll find they were all in contact with Levy."

"We have his phone records, and Sands gave us the computer history of all sent and received e-mails. Not content, but we don't need it. It's a matter of if they were in contact or not."

"And it could show us who else is slated for an accident."

"We must find that. Give me a list as soon as you have it. I'll put it in my file and find a way to protect any other planned victims – if I can find the time. I'm involved in an intense investigation of a serial type killer!"

"Well, I'll look it up. I'll have the list ready ... well, I am also involved in that same intense investigation, so it will have to wait."

They shook hands. There was no smile or grin. Sam went to his desk, Jan went back to the computer. She found the records from Levy's computer and inserted it.

"Found anything?" Sam asked, five and a half hours later. Jan had stayed on the computer, he had talked with several people from forensics and the morgue. He did some research on gardenias, but nothing new, so he started investigating organizations that had gardenias in the name or on a logo. There were a lot of garden clubs, four in the immediate area, that had gardenias on their logo, and one that was called, "Riverside Gardenia Cultivators."

He went to the community center building in the Riverside area. They had contact information, so he called the recording secretary of the club and said he had to get a list of the members of the club. No, it was not about anything criminal that any could be charged with. It was, in fact, about finding information to eliminate those members as suspects. It could well be to protect one or more of them from becoming victims of a crime.

"Samuel Rankin? You are with homicide? You were on television when you caught that man who raped and killed those two women?"

"Yes."

"And you say you wish to protect someone in the club?"

"It's my job to protect everyone in the club, and everyone not in it. As to specific persons, I can't say until I've spoken with them. It is a possibility ... I can't speak about until I have more information."

"You are investigating ... Kate Simples said there was a murder ... two murders, where a gardenia was found?"

"Please! We don't want that knowledge to become general! It's something that could cause someone to slip up, if you know what I mean?"

"Oh! And Kate ... Detective, Kate didn't have anything to do with that!"

"No. The murder was not by a woman. The important thing is that we know where she learned about it."

"Oh, dear! That means she could be in danger?"

"You see. We have to arrange to protect her – if she got the information from someone involved."

"Oh, dear! Of *course* I will cooperate in any way I can! Oh, dear!"

He said he'd come right over to get the list, and please don't say anything to anyone until he had a chance to speak with them. He didn't want to put anyone in danger solely because he talked to them. It must be discreet.

He talked with six of them, nine to go. Tomorrow. Kate's brother was an ambulance driver who overheard two CSI team investigators talking.

"Well, there's, as someone said earlier, an avalanche of information. There's definitely corruption involved. The people who vote for special favors to the drug companies and pesticide companies have millions donated to their campaigns by those companies.

"Sam, we don't just have smoke. We have a raging forest fire. The media won't even mention a lot of it. That's what Jenner and flags and murders in churches are about. They consume all the time and attention, and people don't have a clue as to what's really going on."

"Well, it has to wait until tomorrow. I'm worn out to where I can't hold a thought – Oh! Find anymore likely vics?"

"Four fit the profile. Wilma Farnsworthy, Donald Baines, Robert Moore and Oscar Evans. I'd put my money on Evans. I might try to stop anything happening to the other three. Evans was that big sour-looking man to the left in the meeting. Third from far end. Only thing he said on the video was that they had to find a way to cut out all the waste they were paying for. It hurt the annual report."

"I thought I'd seen him around town. Maybe I'll have the disgusting job of talking to him. Tomorrow. I'm for a long cool shower, a good meal, and sacking out for ten hours or so!"

Adios, Mr. Evans

Sam went into the station in the morning half an hour before his shift was to begin. He sat at his desk to go over a couple of files. Jan came in soon. She talked a bit about the case, then went out to talk with a man who "Might have seen someone" at the restaurant where the food for Levy was prepared. Sam would try to contact Evans.

Evans didn't answer the phone, so Sam sighed and went to his car to drive out to the exclusive section of town. The address was very upscale. There was a BMW and a Lexus in the drive, and a very nice yacht at the dock, which brought a grin to Sam's face. That yacht couldn't go far, upstream or downstream. It was too big for the river.

At the house, no one answered the door. There were two cars in the drive. He called vehicular and soon had the information that Evans had two cars, a BMW and a Lexus.

He didn't have a staff in that mansion?

Sam went around the side and to the back. The door was open. He called, then went inside, into the kitchen. The place was far too quiet.. There was no evidence anyone was there.

Sam called a few more times, then went into the dining room, through to the salon. Evans was laying by the big marble fireplace. A bloody poker was across his chest. His head was a bloody mess.

Sam radioed for the CSI team and investigators. Jan heard the call and said she'd be right there. The description of the man seen by the parking lot to the restaurant was vague, and would fit hundreds of people.

The crew showed up nine minutes later and started their CSI. Sam went out front just as Jan drove up, so they went to the coffee shop four blocks away to have the regular cops' repast: Coffee and donuts. They talked about the case a bit, then went back, just as the body was being put into the ambulance. The CSI head man, John Dobbs, said there wasn't much there. The place was clean. Not any fingerprints that shouldn't be there, but everyone who ever saw a cop show on TV knew about gloves. They had a small spot where the killer stepped in blood, but it wasn't even enough to get a shoe size from.

There was a gardenia, but Sam saw that when he first went into the room.

John waved and got in the ambulance. It

started pulling away.

"Adios, Mr. Evans," Sam said sourly. Jan sighed. They went inside the house.

Jan went into the office/den to the computers. Three of them, top grade. She sat and went through everything there. It wasn't much. They had most of what was concerned with the companies and stocks. There was a lot of porno. DVD's and memory sticks. Evans had been to dozens of porno sites. After about twenty minutes, Jan called Sam in. She showed him some porn videos, and said three of the memory sticks had videos that had been altered, in that they had parts zoomed.

"Sam, he zoomed those pictures up and copied them, I think. Two are just regular porno, one is triple X gay."

"Whiteside?"

"No. Why?"

"Just an idea."

"Well, those videos weren't the commercial things. I mean, they were and they weren't. They were spycam videos. Those show up on the sites at times."

"Oh. Someone in Evans' level was into black-mail – or was Evans one of the subjects?"

"No. He wasn't. I'd about come to the same conclusion. I doubted it, but wondered, then I remembered those board meeting videos."

Sam raised an eyebrow.

"Uh-huh. All three were in that video. He was blackmailing them into voting his way?"

"Were they any of the speakers or where they just there?"

"Just there, but we didn't watch the whole meeting."

Sam nodded. "I think I want to go over the emails between Levy and Evans."

"Yeah. Working together on some scheme where they'd get all the money in the world. Try to fill the hole where other people have a conscience with money.

"Cripes! How can anyone be that damned *empty*!"

They spent another two hours in the house, then took a few items with them to the station. When they compared the memory sticks with other evidence it became plain what they were doing. Part of it was destroying the reputations of people who went against them. Any way they could.

"I know damned well Evans is the one who hired a hit man against those two doctors," Sam said. "He died way too easy to suit me!"

"All of them did! We know who killed them, but not who."

"Yeah. We know the type, motive, and everything else. We don't know the name."

."I intend to find it. I'll want to give them the citizenship medal!"

"There are three more we have to try to protect. I make remarks and can be as cynical as I like, but I also have a sworn duty. I take an oath seriously.

"Do I sound obsequious, or what?"

"Second the motion," Jan made a sour face. "Sam, this won't accomplish anything I can see. Maybe Levy and Evans were the only ones big enough to influence much. The overall votes on those corporate boards won't even notice their absence. It has to be personal. No one could believe a few murders in a town, even as rich as this one, could change the big picture. We have to look for a personal motive, so relatives of the dead doctors ....

"We still have to find a motive."

"We can call on those three. I hope we don't call on three more bodies."

"Yeah. Wilma Farnsworthy, Robert Moore and Donald Baines. I wonder if we'll recognize them from the meeting videos ... but. Shit!"

"What?"

"All those people at the meeting weren't from here. I think we have to know what's going to happen with the stocks our victims held!"

Jan thought for a moment. She had a very sour look on her face. "Somebody killing the others off to get their stocks? I wouldn't blink! Not about that crowd."

"It's gonna be damned hard to keep a straight face when we talk to those three. On the other hand, what if it's somebody not even in this state ... Hell! Not even in this country! This kind of murder can be hired out from anywhere! Baines or Moore or Farnsworthy, probably all clones."

"Shall we call on the lovely sweet Farnsworthy angel?" That one got Jan the bird with a twist.

They had to get past the gate. Jan said they were there to protect Ms. Farnsworthy, that several people in a group she was a member of were dead. The gateman made a couple of calls, then handed the interphone to Sam, who explained that it seemed stockholders of certain big international firms were being murdered. They were there to try to protect her.

"I am quite secure here. I think I am in no danger. I will deny the request. Good day."

"Wait! Consider one thing here."

"I'm quite sure I have considered sufficient options. I am safe. I have things to do, so you *will* excuse me!"

"Oscar Evans. Did he have as good or better security? How about Norton Levy? Are you really that secure?"

There was a growing silence. Sam was just handing the receiver back to the gateman when Farnsworthy said, "Perhaps, just perhaps, you have a point. I will grant you fifteen minutes. Pass the phone to James."

Sam had to bite his tongue. He was about to

tell her she could take her security and shove it up her ass. Jan gave him a warning look. He didn't say anything. He handed the phone to the gateman, who listened, said, "Very well." and threw the switch to open the gate.

Sam drove in. He told Jan about how he was "granted" fifteen minutes, and ordered to "Pass the phone to James."

"Damn it, Jan! You have to sit on me on this! She's is one total RPITA!"

"A what?"

"Royal pain in the ass!"

He parked next to an old Rolls Royce with a uniformed chauffeur polishing the radiator.

"Do you have to live in that uniform in this heat all the time?" Jan asked. A small flicker of a grin crossed his face. He shrugged. "At a thou a week plus room and board, it's worth it. I have to take her somewhere later. I usually leave off the coat if she's not around."

"Is she ... like what she sounded like on the phone?" Sam asked.

"Oh, no! Not at all! She's ten times worse in person!"

They all laughed. He pointed to the huge carved mahogany door, where a uniformed older houseman waited with a look that said very clearly, "You are wasting my valuable time, here!"

Jan sized him up. "Got a corncob up his ass. I thought this kind of thing was only in B movies."

He heard it, of course. She meant for him to. He reddened and pointed inside. They went in to see what looked like an acre of inlaid pink marble floor. The stiff led them to a patio in back with a magnificent view of the river bend across a wide manicured lawn. There was another fancy yacht here. It was also far too large for the river. It had a helicopter sitting on the roof-deck!

A middle-aged, slightly heavy, rather ugly woman in a severe business suit came out onto the patio. Imperially. Her look was total disdain for these peons who were invading her privacy.

She demanded, "What is it you want? What is your business here?"

"That was explained over the telephone a few minutes ago," Jan replied – before Sam could say, "To protect your sorry obnoxious arrogant ass from a serial killer!"

"I feel I am in no danger. No stranger can pass here."

"That is possibly true, but a familiar person can. You hold a lot of control stock that a lot of people *just like you* would like to get their hands on. I don't doubt for a second that you would arrange anyway you could to get your hands on their stocks. Anyway at all. Whatever the situation calls for."

Sam had to suppress a grin at Jan's reply. It hit home with Farnsworthy.

"I see. You think it one of the other stockholders, and have reason! Mr. Evans and Mr. Levy certainly had major blocks of stocks in certain ... ventures."

"Yes. That, too," Jan replied.

"I see. I assure you, I wouldn't know how to arrange such a thing."

"But you were heard to say, on various occasions (he remembered a remark at that meeting. She made it), that one hires an expert to handle any parts of a venture where you have no expertise," Sam said. "Any of you could do that."

Her face hardened. Her eyes narrowed. "I would not know any experts in *that* field!"

"But it would be a matter of suggesting, at one of your meetings, that you would like to know experts in that or any field," Jan suggested. "We are here to advise you that you should take extra precautions until this is resolved, if you are not the person behind it."

Her mouth was a hard, straight line. She didn't

say anything.

"We noted your security arrangements as we entered. That is our expertise. We find it most effective, unless you have not prepared sufficient surveillance from an approach from the river. Do you have motion and sound detection in that area?" Jan looked in her notebook and pretended to write something.

Now Farnsworthy was looking shocked. "I, er, that is, I contracted with a service that is associated with a company in which I hold *substantial* interest. I am sure everything is *quite* proper."

"Well, so long as whoever isn't also a stockholder or whatever. We were to inform you. We did. What you do with the information is your affair. Good afternoon," Sam said. He started for the door, Jan following.

"Officer! A moment! I will contact the service to affirm all areas are secured!"

"We aren't needed for that. Just get guaranteed advice," Jan replied. She and Sam went on through the house and out the front. They got in the car and were by the closed gate. "Open it!" Jan demanded.

"The madam requests that you wait for a moment, until she has received assurances of the matter discussed with yourselves."

"I see. We are being illegally detained. That is known as kidnaping, and you and she will be charged with same," Jan said.

"No! She just asked that you wait! I didn't open the gate because I didn't tell you yet! I'll open it!"

The interphone buzzed. He grabbed it, listened, and hung it up. He was literally sweating.

"The area is secure." He flipped the switch and the gate slid open. Sam drove out.

"Jan, I want to know why he panicked like that."

"I caught that. He does *not* want to be investigated. Probably has a record he doesn't want the lady to know about?"

"It would show how efficient her security company really is, huh?"

"What a way to live! Can't trust anyone, because she can't be trusted. Spend her whole life in that ostentatious mausoleum. You can have it!"

"Quite frankly, My Dear, I wouldn't want it."

"Well, I hope Baines and Moore aren't quite as assholey."

"Assholey?"

"Sort of sounds appropriate."

"Can't argue that."

<u>*Surprise!*</u>

Moore wasn't home. He often wasn't available for periods when the *tremendous* pressures of business necessitated a time to relieve the blah, blah, blah. They could ask for an appointment and could speak with him, say, Tuesday, at three ten? He had half an hour unscheduled then. Mr. Moore did not meet with anyone without an appointment. Period. He was a very busy, very important business leader.

"We'll wait until he's home and deliver a court order. He can argue with the judge about appointments with those who are trying to save his life."

The super-efficient secretary was staring at them in shock when they walked out. Jan said she went to high school with a prig just like her. A snooty phony snob without a pot or window. Bureaucratic thinker. "See how powerful I am? You can't talk with my *very* powerful boss unless I say you can!"

They drove to Eastpoint, to a really nice upper-middle class place on the river. A man saw them drive in and called he was in the back lawn, working on the azaleas.

"Mr. Baines? We need to talk to you about the recent killings of people involved with stocks in companies you also hold voting stocks in." Jan felt it best she do the introduction bit. Sam would not react well to the type of people, so far.

"Oh, damn! I thought it would take longer than this to catch me!"

"*What*?!"

He laughed. "I know all about it. I sure as Hell am not surprised! I can think of one or two more who should go the route of the failed investor. The world would be better off."

Baines had a very nice place. It was a long way from the others, being more a normal upscale family place. He was in the garden surrounding a picturesque greenhouse that was designed to look like a guest cabin. They could see colorful orchids through the open door. A brown pea gravel path led to the teak dock, where a 16' fishing boat was moored. Two teenagers were just coming from the dock, carrying a stringer with a couple of bass. Baines introduced them as Donny and Frankie. He said they were neigh-borhood kids. Raised right. Good, solid family. They waved and went on.

"You have children?" Sam asked.

"No. I did. A wonderful wife and a son and daughter. They died nine years ago, in India. They were there when the Camel Flu went through. More than eleven thousand people died there. They were on vacation while I was working with the oil exploration team in Yemen."

"I hadn't heard about that one!" Jan cried.

"Wasn't big enough to get international attention. Only lasted three weeks, but took a heavy toll. They contained it. They vaccinated everyone when it first broke out, but that was, if anything, what made it worse.

"I'd prefer to talk of other matters?"

"Yes. Sorry," Sam said. "We're investigating the murders. All the victims held control stock in three companies that you have same. We have to warn you that those stocks seem to be the only connection among the victims."

"Yeah. I went to a couple of meetings where they were. I certainly didn't care to socialize with that kind of greedy soulless bunch. Not one little joke or even a flicker of a grin among them. I didn't go to any meetings after the first couple. They knew I was going to vote against most of it. They would have thanked me for *not* attending.

"That was three years ago. I inherited a lot of

stock from my grandfather. He was a little like that type, but was never that extreme. He wanted a lot of money, but there were limits to what he would do to get it.

"They have no limits."

"We have a theory there is someone who is acting like they act. Someone who wants their stocks and will do anything to get them. If knocking them off is called for, that's the situation. Go for it!" Jan said.

"That describes them. Their lives are big empty holes they try to fill with money. They can't see the more money they pour into the hole, the deeper and darker it gets."

"Like Clint Faraday says, they don't own the money. It owns them," Sam said.

"Very true. Who the Hell is Clint Faraday?"

"He's the hero in a murder mystery series. Do you have any ideas about who the killer could be?"

"Judging by personality, it could be any one of hundreds in those companies. All the top echelon.

"They wouldn't do it unless they figured a way to not get caught, because too much could come out about the companies if it gets a lot of publicity, meaning the value of their stocks would plummet. What good would it do if they got tons of stocks no one would buy? Who would buy it if part of the deal is you get knocked over?

"They're also the type that would keep their mouths shut if they know, for the same reason."

"You wouldn't believe some of the things we found in their records, particularly computer records, complete with video," Jan said. "One we contacted said she had perfect security and was immune from that kind of attack. Sam asked her if Levy and Evans had as good a security system. She pissed in her royal panties, I think."

"Yes I would. I said there is nothing below them. The whole world's turning into them, anymore. They own and run the country.

"Don't get me on my soapbox! I'll rant and rave your ears off!

"I can assume you met the super-high queen of the bitch world, the ugly and untalented Miss Farnsworthy your royal higher-that-highness, you lowly serf trash?"

They laughed. Sam said he agreed with him in every department, so far. He was preaching to the choir.

"I do *not* preach! Religion is just one of their tools!"

He offered them iced tea or beer. He wouldn't tell if they took the beer.

Sam took a beer, Jan iced tea. They chatted for more than two hours. Baines let a lot of things about the companies slip without knowing he did so. He would never own one share of those companies if he didn't inherit them. He wouldn't own any stocks in any companies if he hadn't inherited them. He wasn't the stocks and bonds type. Evans and Levy pulled some very underhanded things, Moore was an old-school gangster type who suddenly ended up with a lot of stocks when his father and uncle were killed in some kind of mafia war or something. He seemed to be trying to go legit, but there were a lot of questions. He was suspected of corrupting politicians, of intimidating them.

They agreed with much of it. Don was a great surprise, after the others.

When they were headed back to the station, Sam said they had, at least, eliminated one suspect. They could be sure it wasn't Baines.

"How do you figure?" Jan asked.

"Farnsworthy. The way he hates that woman, she would have been first. Very slow and very painful. It seemed, at times, that he held her personally responsible for his family, which could mean he knows something about her, probably subconsciously, that could mean she really is behind it."

Jan looked thoughtful, then slowly nodded.

"Well. I've been on the internet most of the afternoon," Jan reported. "I checked on that Camel flu thing and got involved. I couldn't believe what those companies are and what they're doing!

"Sam, there's a lot of evidence that the Camel flu was the result of the vaccinations. It was a rare thing until a big campaign to eradicate it was run by the country's health commission. It could be fatal in about two percent of the cases, which amounted to four or five people a year. The commission bought the vaccine and gave the shots to all the foreigners coming into the test area and to all the people in the area. It looked fine for two weeks, then people started getting the flu by the hundreds, then thousands. Twenty thousand people were injected. Four thousand two hundred thirty one died from the flu. The only ones who survived had a pro-bability of being exposed to the flu and had a natural immunity.

"The government got sued, and paid the families of the ones who died ten thousand dollars each, and it was hushed up. The drug companies made two million dollars from the vaccine and were fined forty thousand dollars.

"Sam, that was a small one. The vaccines today don't have that bad a record – in the short term.

"If the charges are exaggerated five hundred percent, the answer is still intolerable! I can't believe it!

"You know what this means?"

"Yeah. Don. I don't buy it. Farnsworthy would be long gone by now. There has to be something we've missed."

"No shit?" He gave her the finger.

"Jan, it doesn't make sense. Don wouldn't ... well, he would, but not this way. He would see them all as guilty, but would go after the bitch queen first, and it would be slow and painful. He would want to make it last. It just doesn't figure.

"We've said before that it could be anyone in that bracket, and that they'd hire it out.

"Those gardenias have to figure into it. I didn't see any around Don's place, which doesn't mean much. There could be all two hundred forty species there. He's got about ten acres, and it's all gardens. We saw a very small part of it."

"Well, there was a big one on the corner where we turned in there of the type at the scenes. *Gardenia lucida*. Maybe *gumminifera*. They're almost the same. There was even an argument in the Botanical Society of India about how to tell them apart, or if they were the same species.

"Cripes! Now I'm an expert on gardenias? Am I going to ... Sam! They're from India!"

"I don't see ... another connection to Dan? I hope not!"

"I'm going to research that gardenia like it's never been researched before. There has to be something ... a connection, somehow, with something. Or someone.

"Sam, think about this: Farnsworthy wants all that stock. She knows how Don hates the sight of her. She knows he was in India – or his family was – and what happened. She would, naturally, be the one he would go after, and ... it's fallen apart, right?"

Sam sighed and stared at the top of his desk while tapping himself on the head with a ballpoint pen. He looked up, smirked, and said, "How clever would that be? I wonder! Just exactly how clever would that be?

"Try this: she wants all that stock. She see's Baines as an obstacle while he's alive. She wants to turn that liability into an asset. She has to get rid of the others and have him blamed.

"How does she do it?

"Leave something at each scene that points to Baines!

"What would that be? It would have to be

subtle, but something that would get our attention, something that would lead to him, and nobody else.

"He hates her because he believes she had something to do with his wife and kids dying in India from something her drug company ... you know what I mean.

"How can she do that?

"Subtle. Gardenias, India.

"That means we have to find something that connects Baines to gardenias and India. She also has to come up with something that will make it seem natural that he didn't go after her.

"Well, the stock holdings of all the victims would be known, and that would be a connection, so the stupid cops would, naturally, contact her, as she was a major holder of all three stocks.

"How could she do that? How could she connect that with anything? Something that would make us think Baines didn't go after her because he couldn't find any way!

"So we go to her place and come across a security setup that would mean he couldn't go after her. He couldn't hope to get to her.

"Incidentally, I looked up George Hilton, the gateman. He's possibly hiding from a loan company in Montana, which doesn't concern us.

"It had to be solid. That would be why we were stopped when we were leaving. We hadn't shown for sure that he couldn't breach her security. There was an area we might have doubts about, so we were stopped at the gate, she called and told the gateman that she had checked with the security company, and the entire area was covered? She didn't have time to have called them, for them to check their plots and tell her it was covered!

"Make any sense?"

"In a way. I wondered why anyone would be so stupid as to make us think they could keep us there..

"Sam, that still doesn't make the connection with gardenias."

"I think, if you'll check, there is a connection. It's in India, but can be checked from here. It will be something that concerns him and no one else."

"I think it's worth a shot. I think I'm going to find it, but not let out a hint."

"Because?"

"Because it won't work if we don't make the connection, will it?"

Sam laughed a humorless laugh. "So she'll have to make damned sure we know of the connection."

"Dju godt it!"

She went to her computer and started trying searches on gardenia/india. That got all the sites she'd already searched.

She tried gardenia/india/provinces. She got that they grew in all provinces.

She tried several others, then gardenia/india/business names. That gave a list that she added logos to, which shortened the list a little.

She may have something, but it didn't seem quite right.

She thought, then called, "Sam? Did Don say where in India his wife and kids were staying, where they got the vaccinations?"

Sam shrugged. He looked up Don's number and called.

"Don? Sam, I hate to have to ask this, but where in India were your family?"

"Where? Sikkim and Jadharta. They were going to see a little of China, then meet me to come back to the states. Got any new leads?"

"I have a few questions to ask. I don't like the way that vaccination program worked. At all. I never knew ... I never heard of that and several other 'tests' run by those companies."

"Now, if someone bombed those companies off the face of the Earth, you could be damned certain I was number one on the suspect list!"

They chatted a minute, then Sam told Jan the provinces. She went to the computer and tried several things, then whistled.

"Paydirt?"

"You could say that. It didn't come up when I checked the vaccinations.

"Want a guess at what center of health made the injections on two thousand people in Sikkim?"

"Gardenia something?"

"No. Health Services of Sikkim. However, there was a code name used there for the test. Project, in translation, White Fragrant Flower. That was the local name of *Gardenia lucida*.

"So now that we stupid cops haven't made what has to be an obvious connection, she has to cause us to make a connection.

"How do you think she'll manage that?"

"Considering that we haven't let out that there was anything about gardenias in the investigation, she has to assume we aren't saying anything so we can trap someone."

"How will she handle it?"

"I don't know. She'll think of something. It will have to be soon."

They chatted a bit, then went to lunch. Nothing happened the rest of the day that had anything to do with the case.

Sam and Jan were making out a schedule for tracking a rapist the next morning when Jan was called to the phone.

"Yes? Detective Jameson here."

"Detective, I am Miss Farnsworthy. You and some other detective came to my home yesterday to ask insulting questions ... I suppose that is your job. I tend to be overly sensitive, in certain instances."

"What do you want?" She let a sharpness creep into her voice.

"Something has happened that has made me uncomfortable. Something that I feel is connected to the reason you were here."

Jan waited a few seconds. "And?"

"It is about the security."

"I am not a mindreader. What?"

"Well, it seems that, er, as you suggested, there may be a breach in the system, or, at least, it appears that it was breached sometime last night."

"Call the security company and demand an explanation. Was something stolen? Property damaged? Call burglary, or I can transfer."

"No! It wasn't that! Nothing was damaged, but a threat ... of a kind. I am fearful it may be about the stockholder deaths. I can conceive of no other reason for it, and I don't understand! Gardenias? I don't know why someone would illegally enter my house and grounds to simply leave a gardenia on the guest book!"

"A gardenia? On the guest book? You don't make any sense! Why would anyone leave a gardenia if they broke into your house? Only to prove your security was not as good as you thought? You don't make any sense, Miss Farnsworthy, and that is not in the province of this department. We deal with violent crimes."

She raised a thumb. Sam smirked.

"Oh, please! It may be because of a, er, test, you see, that a company in which I hold a *very* small portfolio, you understand, of voting stock ... a test that went horribly wrong, and some testees were, uh, slightly, uh, damaged. It was in India, which is why I can't see how ... it was called, if you translate from Hindi, the White Gardenia Project. In Sikkim. A, um, health issue thing.

"You see, someone may believe I acted un-wisely while recommending the project. I was just one of those who urged the project. I mean, it *had* to be tested!"

"How would that connect to ... oh. The others backed you in the vote?"

"Er, well, that is, you see...."

"We can determine if anyone affected by that test – what did you call it? The White Gardenia Project – is in this area. I have to admit there are people who would seek revenge on such a matter. That would mean they or their family were damaged in the test. Thank you for calling. I would suggest you contact your security service and, please excuse the vernacular, raise unholy hell. I imagine the service isn't cheap. You deserve what you are paying for."

"Er, yes. I will do that. Thank you." She rung off.

"Well, Sam! She didn't only tell us there was a connection to find, she pointed out exactly where and what the connection is!"

"She's about a tenth as clever as she thinks she is. The lady, excuse the expression, has a much too high opinion of herself and her abilities."

"So now we have to come up with something that proves it. She hired it done, I suppose – I know. We have to find who she hired and break them down."

"Which could mean she gets away with it."

"She has to do something to stop us from going

past the surface, which means she doesn't have a choice. She has to go after Don."

"She does?"

"If he's alive and well, he can probably prove at least one place he couldn't have committed the murder. If he's dead, we'll mark the case closed."

"We will?"

"Well, wouldn't that be a lot easier than spending all that time and effort actually investigating anything?"

They did a palm slap.

Now, it was a matter of protecting Baines. A hired killer would come after him. They wanted to be there.

It would have to be done before they started any deeper investigation than would be done after they determined Baines was the only one with a connection. They were already a step ahead of her on this. They would have to stay ahead or someone else would end up dead while the way to prove who a killer, or who hired that killer, was would go down the toilet.

Sam called Baines to warn him. Don said it wouldn't surprise him if any one of that crowd hired killers to protect their investments. He knew a few little tricks, himself, as they would learn. He agreed to carry a locator that would call them with exactly where he was if he was in danger. They would never be far. He said nobody would come there, so maybe they should tap his phone, in case someone called with a way to get him to go somewhere.

Then, all they could do was wait. They didn't think it would be long.

They went back to the rapist case. About two hours later they got a beeper alert. Don was receiving a call he thought was suspicious, so they listened to Farnsworthy saying that there was to be a secret meeting at Moore's place. It was about the recent deaths of members of the investment group. Don said he wasn't a member of any investment group. He just had a few stocks. She said his having those stocks might mean he was in great danger. They had to get together to find a way to protect themselves until they could be guaranteed safety. He said he wasn't in any danger. He wasn't active with that crap and wasn't about to become active. It ended when he said he would go to Moore's place a bit later. Where was it?

She rang off, and Don said,"Sam? Jan?"

"Yeah. both of us," Jan replied. "Rather a strange call, eh what?"

"I didn't really think she was behind anything until that. What do you think they'll do?"

"I don't know. I'd recommend you don't go to ... maybe call Moore and arrange to meet in a public place?" Sam suggested.

"That might work, but I don't know how to call him. I don't have his private number."

"Then don't go."

"Oh, I'll go. I'm capable of protecting myself, particularly when they don't know I suspect anything."

They finally said they would be close, and would listen on the tap. Be careful – and armed. They knew he had a permit for a pistol. Take it with him.

He said it wouldn't be necessary ... but, then, Moore was a hood, so ... okay. Just to be safe,

He would show up fifteen minutes early. Throw their timing off.

Sam and Jan got an unmarked and headed to the fork of the road where Don would turn into Moore's drive. They could just see the front of Moore's house. There was a Rolls Royce they had seen before parked in front.

Jan smirked. "Seems Farnsworthy plans to be early, too." Sam laughed.

Ten minutes later Farnsworthy went to her car and it left. Sam raised an eyebrow.

A few minutes later the locator came on that showed Don was close. He drove into the drive, paused, and went on. He stopped just before the parking space, then went on around the house.

"What's that about?" Jan asked.

The audio came on. Don said, very quietly, "I'm to go around and to the dock, to the yacht? What the hell is that about ... oh, right. She doesn't want to be seen, I suppose."

They had no way to reply. Don went out of sight around the house. Sam started the engine. They heard Don's car park and the door slam, then the sounds of him walking on the gravel path, then he called that he was there.

A voice mumbled something, He answered that he would come on aboard, then, "What the *Hell*? What are you ...!" and a shot.

Sam spun out and raced around the house and down to slide to a stop next to Don's car. Don was standing on the gangplank, just at the deck rail. Jan was running toward him, Sam right behind her, both with their Glocks drawn.

Don was standing over the body of a bullish man. There was blood under the body.

"My God! He had ... my God!"

There was an old Army Colt .45 about three feet from the body's hand.

"I was a little faster than him," Don said, drily. "I didn't know what to expect, so I had my thirty eight in my hand in my pocket."

"Forty five," Jan said. "I wonder! Will a ballistic test tell us if that gun killed anyone else?"

Don seemed bewildered. Sam radioed for the CSI team. The secretary from yesterday was running toward them. Jan stopped her and asked why Moore was at the yacht, not in his office in the house.

"He got a call on his personal line and came down here! What happened?!"

"He tried to *kill* me!" Don cried.

They held the secretary back. The CSI van soon came. Jan, Don and the secretary went to the house. Sam watched as the team carefully photographed the scene and surrounding area. Will then turned the body over and went through the pockets. There was a cell phone in a belt holder. Sam checked, but the last three calls he'd received didn't have a caller ID number. Private.

There was an envelope in the shirt pocket. It was a stock assignment to his account. Two hundred shares of World Life Guarantee, and Investment Insurance company, value: $1,214/ shr. A quarter of a million dollars. It was to be transferred from the account of Wilma Farnsworthy for value received. There was a note in the envelope – *last one, Bob! This will complete it. Good work! – Wilma F.* The note was handwritten.

"Mean anything?" Will asked.

"Oh, yeah!" Sam replied.

"... will show exactly where and why things happened as they did. The murders of at least five people and the death of a hired killer have been shown to have eventuated because of a totally greedy person who wanted to increase her more than one *billion* dollar holdings. If murdering people for their stocks was required, that's just business. We have shown that, and more.

"Prosecution rests."

DA Gerry Felstein sat. Donna Atworth, defense attorney, stood, shook her head, and declared, "This is a contrived case. Miss Farnsworthy did *not* hire any killer. The very idea is ludicrous. She is a vastly wealthy woman with no *reason* to have anyone killed. She could buy any of the stocks those people held.

"We will show that this case was one of planted evidence or simply misinterpreted evidence that was taken out of context by an overzealous prosecutor.

"I did not plan to call many witnesses to refute the imaginings of the prosecution.

"I will not take the witnesses in chronological order. It will not be necessary.

"Call Alice Dendry."

The secretary from Moore's came to sit in the witness box and take the oath.

"Miss Dendry, did Mr. Moore own a pistol? An old Colt forty five army pistol?"

"No. I never saw him with any pistol."

"Can you explain the note allegedly found in an envelope in Mr. Moore's possession at the time of his death?"

"Yes. Mr. Moore traded stock in the insurance company for stocks in other of his holdings on three occasions I knew about, because I registered them. That transfer was the final one, where Mr. Moore attained all the stocks in the company Miss Farnsworthy held."

"Why was Mr. Moore on the yacht?"

"He received a call on his private phone. He said it was a business partner, and they had to discuss a sale of stock he wanted."

"Who made that call?"

"I can't say. I was not privy to anything to do with his personal phone."

"I see. You can't say if it was from Miss Farnsworthy or someone else?"

"No. She always called on the office line so there would be a record. That is just business."

"Did Mr. Moore have an appointment with Mr. Baines at that time?"

"No."

"Thank you. Your witness, prosecution."

Felstein went to stand in front of the witness box, shook his head, read a paper, then said, "Did you know of Mr. Moore's early life, his family situation, his police record?"

"Yes. He wanted nothing more to do with that time."

"He was a mafia son with a lot of minor charges, mostly of thuggery, that were subsequently dropped or altered to lesser charges, as outlined in prosecution.

"You say he owned no pistol? That you can state this as fact?"

"Yes. He wanted no connection with his earlier life."

"How many times were you aboard that yacht, and did you, personally, examine each cabin?"

"Relevance!" Atworth shouted.

"Counselor?" from Judge Collins.

"Witness has claimed victim had no pistol. He was aboard the yacht. There was a pistol found at the scene. That pistol was shown to be one used in a murder of a fellow stockholder. The only fingerprints on that pistol were his. I think it is very relevant."

"Continue."

"Miss Dendry?"

"I was never aboard the yacht."

"And you stated there were other transactions involved where the note was concerned. Recently?"

"Well, yes. Within the past month."

"And they were all value received?"

"They were for other stocks."

"Value received, or listed?"

"Er, value received."

"And was each such transaction close in time to a murder of another stockholder?

"Nothing further at this time."

"Objection!" from Atwood. Farnsworthy screeched.

"Grounds?"

"Question was not answer ... withdrawn."

Felstein smirked at Sam and Jan. Nobody said anything while Atwood whispered animatedly with Farnsworthy, until Collins said, "Defense? Anything further?"

"Yes. Call Miss Wilma Farnsworthy!"

"Is she nuts!?" Sam asked Jan.

Farnsworthy marched regally to the witness box, took the oath with a look of utter disdain, and sat.

"I resent this! You will pay dearly for inconveniencing me and publicly humiliating me in this manner. It is unacceptable, and you will regret it! Deeply! Do you know who I *am*?"

"You are a defendant, charged with multiple hirings to commit murder!" Collins snapped. "You will answer questions that are asked, when asked. Another such threatening outbreak and I will recess this action for the ninety days you will sit in a cell for contempt of court! Is that *quite* clear?"

"That is ridiculous! I did *not* hire anyone to commit murder!"

"It appears quite to the contrary, at this time," Felstein said. "May we proceed, Your Honor?"

Farnsworthy looked aghast. She was about to say something. Collins said, "One more word!" Farnsworthy tightened her lips and glared.

"I advised my client against taking the stand," Atwood said. "I have no questions of pertinence here. I may merely ask her if she, at any time, in any way, arranged for or hired murder. Her answer was given in her outbreak.

"Miss Farnsworthy, the most damaging accusation is that note. It may be taken in several ways. Please explain that note, and why it was in the possession of Mr. Moore at that particular moment in time."

"I already told you ... very well. I had an

agreement with Mr, Moore to exchange stocks in insurance companies for ... other stocks I wished to acquire to add to my *very extensive* portfolio. He had recently received some of the particular stocks, in pharmaceutical companies, that I wished to acquire. He called me to say he had the stock, that it would finalize my control of ... er, it would finalize a stock option acquisition.

"I had an appointment to meet with him on another business matter, so went earlier to handle that transference. While I was there, the other appointment canceled. I went back to my home."

"Why was the stock transference for value received?"

"We always did that. It means nothing."

"And who was the canceled appointment supposed to be with?" She seemed triumphant.

"Donald Baines, the person who *murdered* Mr. Moore!"

"So! Baines makes an appointment, cancels it, then shows up to kill Moore? Rather strange, would you say?"

"Yes, I would say that!"

"Nothing further! You may step down!"

"I think perhaps that is not within your province to say, Counselor. Witness, you may *not* yet step down," Collins warned. "Prosecution? Cross?"

"This is the first I heard about any canceled appointment. I would like to ask Mr. Baines about that, your honor. Then I would continue with cross? If the court pleases?"

"Mr. Baines, you are still under oath," Collins replied.

Don stood. Felstein asked why he didn't tell him he had canceled the appointment.

"I didn't. I was actually almost fifteen minutes early to the appointment."

"He called me on my private number and canceled!" Farnsworthy screeched.

"How would I even know your private number? You're dingy!" Baines snapped back.

Collins rapped the gavel. "Anything further, Prosecution?"

"Rest."

"Defense?"

"Miss Farnsworthy! Did you not report to me that the meeting was canceled by Mr. Baines *before* going to Mr. Moores home for the transference?"

"Yes!"

"How convenient," Felstein said, drily. "Is counselor calling herself as witness?"

Collins rapped the gavel. "Summation, if

desired?"

"Defer," Felstein said.

Atwood stood, posed and postured before the jury, smirked, rolled her eyes, and walked back and forth while reading a paper. Collins said, pointedly, "Proceed, Counselor!"

"We have a contrived case based on falsified planted evidence here. We have found nothing to base who and why someone would do this to my client. She is merely a successful business-woman in a world dominated by males!

"We have determined that Mr. Baines, the actual murderer here, was deeply involved in a matter in India, where there was an unfortunate experience with a medical problem that affected his family, and he blamed that on my client. We have shown ...."

"Counselor! You are presenting unconfirmed evidence in a summation?" Judge Collins snapped. "If this was your defense, why was it not presented at the proper time? You are a millimeter from disbarment!"

"Your honor ... I wasn't allowed by my client to produce that evidence or to question on it! I had this written up, but she refused to allow it at the last moment!"

"Then don't present it here! Jury will not consider evidence or charges not produced during the trial."

Atwood looked at the pad in her hand. "I do not believe my client killed anyone." She went back to the defense table.

"Mistrial! I demand a mistrial!" Farnsworthy screeched.

"On the grounds that you refused your counselor introduction of evidence? How droll," Collins replied. "You can't call for mistrial. Your attorney would have to do that. You don't have grounds, Mrs. Atwood.

"Prosecution? You deferred?"

"Not necessary. Our case is proven. We would like to know why the defendant refused presenting of evidence that would, supposedly, exonerate her, but I guess that will never be.

"We may assume it would place her into the position her actions have placed many others to reveal what is truly behind this. It is a situation of her own making."

"You said no summation, but I will let that pass as a summation. It also exceeded what may be presented in summation, but I guess it would come down to tit for tat," Collins said, then turned to give the jury instructions.

Don, Sam and Jan went to a local restaurant for a little sustenance while they waited for the jury to return. There was no doubt, whatever, that their decision would be what it was. Guilty on all counts.

Collins set sentencing for Monday at nine AM. They went home.

Don, Sam and Jan left the courtroom where Farnsworthy got 20 years without possibility of parole, laughing and joking. They went to sit in Don's gardens with a cool vodka Collins, to celebrate.

"That lawyer, Atwood, gave me a bit of a scare for a minute," Sam said. "I thought she was going to get that your family was wiped out by a company she had stock in, and that would have made a mess out of it, in that it would bring in reasonable doubt, and you were the only other choice for the killer."

"It would make it even stronger if they checked and found that little bunch were the ones who pushed the vote over the line. If they hadn't voted block, they would have held the testing back another six months. It probably would have never been done, because their test pigs or whatever would have all died."

"They would?" Jan asked. "I didn't know that!"

"I wouldn't have known it if I didn't get that stock, so could check the minutes of those meetings.."

"Why in Hell didn't she bring it up!? The least it would do would be to reduce the sentence!" Jan cried.

"I can figure that!" Sam said. "Remember those eight dead doctors – who were exposing those very companies?"

"I consider that perfect karma or whatever you call it," Don said. "The very kind of trap she created did her in. Her only recourse to avoid spending the rest of her life in the pen would mean she didn't have much of a rest of her life. It was entirely her own doing. It was all of their own doing. No one could ask for a more poetic justice than what we got!

"Well, now that my family is avenged, I'm thinking of getting married again, but I worry about whether my kids will be forced to be vaccinated with the same shit that killed my first family."

"Maybe people will wake up and stop that. It's against the constitution as well as outside the bounds of the war crimes laws," Jan suggested.

"We can hope. I know I'm going after the rest of those companies' directors, if in a different way. I think they can't stand the publicity I'm going to bring them!"

"I think I'll join you in that!" Jan said. "I

wouldn't go so far as to start knocking them off, but I'll sure as sunset try to stop them!"

"Sometimes knocking them off is the only thing that will work. Maybe now they'll realize they aren't above the law and that they don't have a tenth as much security as they thought."

"Security?" Sam asked.

Don laughed. "Perfect security, then somebody waltzes into their living room and leaves a gardenia on the guest book?"

Jan laughed.

Sam wondered; How did Baines know about that gardenia on the guest book? No one had mentioned one word about it where he could have heard!

Well ... let it lie. Like it or not, justice was done here.

"Care to finish the bottle? About three shots left!"

They poured the shots, toasted to the future, and tossed them down.

C. D. Moulton's works are available on most major outlets as printed or e-books. CD writes the CD Grimes, PI, mysteries, the Det. Lt. Nick Storie mysteries, the Clint Faraday mysteries, the Flight of the Maita science fiction series, books on orchid culture and many others of many types. Mystery, adventure, intrigue, science fiction, humor, fantasy, paranormal, mild erotica, and factual.

www.ingramcontent.com/pod-product-compliance
Lightning Source LLC
Chambersburg PA
CBHW050559160726
48003CB00002B/958